Spooky Poems Aloud

For Charlie

WIDE EYED EDITIONS

INTRODUCTION

Beware! This poetry collection
is spooky. There are poems in here
about werewolves and zombies!
Vampires and sludge monsters!
Ghosts and ghouls! Are you feeling
brave? Dare you turn the page?
If you do, not only will I show you
some spoooooky poems, I will also
share the secrets for how you can
write your very own poems to
scare and spook.

Read on, if you dare...

LIMERICKS OF FEAR

Limericks are traditionally read to make people laugh. Have a practice reading these poems to yourself. When you feel confident reading them, try reading aloud to a friend. See if you can make them laugh at these funny but creepy poems.

THE DARK POND

Young Charlie was scared of the park,
with its pond all gloomy and dark.
He poked it with a stick
and with one monstrous lick
was swallowed right up by a shark!

THE POO OF DEATH

Little David needed the loo,
but inside lurked an evil poo.
He tried in a rush
to give it a flush
but got covered in icky brown goo.

THE TOOTHED LIBRARY

Wise Sabina loved the library;
the only place where she felt free.
But on one fateful night
the old shelves took a bite
and swallowed her up totally!

THE MOULDY LUNCH BOX

Amira found an old lunch box
in the playground, under some rocks.
When she opened the thing,
mould covered her skin
and wrapped her from head to socks.

IT WOKE ME FROM A DREAM

This poem has a **repeating line** that is very creepy,
"Waiting, watching", and at the end of the poem the line
becomes even creepier. Can you write a poem with a creepy
repeating line?

It woke me from a dream
with its shuffling.

Opening one sleep-smeared eye
I spy it: fat, squat and dark
in the corner of my room.
Waiting, watching.

I slam my eyelids tight,
curl my legs within
the castle of my covers.
But I feel it there.
Waiting, watching.

"What do you want?" I ask
into my room's dark mouth
as the moonlight traces its silhouette.
Waiting, watching.

"Have you come because of what I did?"
I whisper into my sweat-soaked pillow.
No reply hisses back,
but still, it's there.
Waiting, watching.

"I'll make it okay", I say.
"I'll say sorry, I'll right the wrong",
and slowly, it slithers away whispering,
"I'll be waiting, watching".

THE TOWER

How can a place be scary?
Can you create a poem about a scary
building, street, house or park.
What words can you use to create an
eerie **atmosphere**? In this poem, much
of the tension is created by the way the
narrator responds to the places.
How will your narrator respond to the
scary location you create?

The tower block was empty
but its dark windows
seemed to stare.

The boarded-up lifts and
stairwells
seemed to whisper "come".
The tumbled shopping trolleys
seemed to clatter a laugh.

We sit silent on our bikes,
looking up at its towering height.
Its aerials seemed to point,
its rusted satellite dishes
seemed to listen.

We try to cycle away,
to leave its cold concrete
embrace,
but its chill seeps into us and...

...we seem to be inside.
We seem to be looking down
on two bikes
abandoned in its shadow.

THE SATYR'S HEAD

The hidden garden we played in
was bordered in red brick.
Crenelations of a faded fort,
Ivy-scarred and wind-aged.
A Victorian garden.

The towering walls tempted us to climb,
the bricks testing their mortar,
forming steps and hand-holds.

We climbed.
Urging frail frames against the height,
then daring to drop to the spiky grass below.
Protected by a wisp of arrogance,
an armour of childhood.

We danced in the light of the satyr's grin,
the limestone detail of the fountain,
weathered and mean,
the endless grimace of a fiend.

The garden cloaked our tower block's stares,
its trees veiling the aerials, the satellite dishes.
Its bricks, a smoke screen to the traffic's roar, the yells of our mothers.
Its bushes covering up the smog.
The jam-sweet scent of winter berries
disguising the stench from the bins.

We danced liked our fathers told us we could,
spinning in the dead leaves
that spun from our steps
like charred circus performers.

ON A COLD, WHISPERING NIGHT

This is a poem to be **whispered** into the ear of
a friend or fiend, designed to scare them senseless!
How many people will you scare?

On a cold, whispering night
as the clouds swallowed the stars,
as the moon peeped its light
between the trees' dancing scars.

A tall figure came a-floating
through the cold cobbled streets.
No face seen in its darkness
no steps heard from its feet.

No shadow even cast
by the moon's cautious light.
No breath even heard
on this cold whispering night.

No utterance was given
as it lifted a bony hand,
as it pointed a crooked finger
at the falling sand...

...that tumbled in the hourglass
hung from its hooded neck
nearly all fallen
except for one last speck.

One grain of gritty midnight,
one iota of dust.
The figure spoke inside my head,
"It's time to join us".

As that last fragment fell,
as shadow swallowed my light,
I began my own wanderings,
on that cold whispering night.

CLUB RULES

Here are the rules to join two clubs, Werewolf Club and Vampire Club. Can you make up the rules for other monster clubs? What are the rules for Zombie Club? Everyone must eat brains? What are the rules for Loch Ness Club? No photos allowed? What are the rules for Witch Club? Be sure to know which, witch is which?

MEAT NOT SWEETS

NO CATS

WW ONLY

DO NOT ENTER!

N
CH
TO

WEREWOLF CLUB RULES

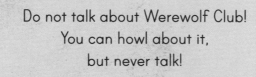

Do not talk about Werewolf Club!
You can howl about it,
but never talk!

Do not walk to Werewolf Club!
You can bound to it in moonlight,
but never walk!

Do not eat sweets at Werewolf Club!
You can eat meat, raw meat,
but no sweets!

Do not bring cats to Werewolf Club!
You can bring bats, hats and even rats,
but no cats!

Do not bring silver to Werewolf Club!
You can bring gold or pewter or even bronze,
but no silver!

Do not bring chewy toys to Werewolf Club!

If you do they will be confiscated.

You won't get them back.

They are very squeaky
and make it hard
for us to hear the day's agenda!

VAMPIRE CLUB RULES

There are many rules to follow
if you want to join our club.
The first is that each member
must only slurp on blood.

The second is: NO STAKES.
Or things with pointy ends.
Even a sharpened pencil
will be sure to lose you friends.

The third relates to garlic
hiding in a dish.
A vampire may meet their end
from just the merest whiff.

The fourth is to be careful
when flying as a bat.
No one appreciates
a bat splat-attack!

The fifth is NO NOISE
during daylight hours.
A vampire needs her rest
to get her full vampiric powers.

The sixth is NO FAMILIARS
can enter the vampire den.
Familiars get too familiar,
their grovelling knows no end.

The seventh is most important...

...it relates to fun at night.
Be sure to give everyone
a great big monstrous FRIGHT!

ZOMBIE MEMORIES

In this poem I decided to remove a line in each stanza, so that each stanza gets shorter as you make your way through the poem. I wanted to tell the story of a zombie falling apart but as I wrote, it became a sad love story! See if you can write a spooky poem where each verse is one line shorter than the last. You could make it about a skeleton losing its bones, or maybe a witch losing her ingredients for a special potion.

My zombie head is foul and rotting,
my zombie chest reveals a dead black heart,
my zombie arms are crooked and bent,
my zombie waist makes a grating click,
my zombie knees are flapping about,
my zombie feet are twisted.

My zombie memories are decaying away.
The one I loved with my beating heart.
The way we embraced with grasping arms.
The way we danced with swaying hips.
and kicked with joyful knees...

...my zombie feet twist off.

My zombie memories offer up crumbs
of "I love you", with hand on heart.
Us walking the sands, arms interlinked
and running into the surf up to our waists...

...my zombie knees flap off.

My zombie mind tries to hold on
to the way my beating heart broke –
my arms lifting to my face, crooked and bent...

...my zombie waist crumbles off.

My zombie thoughts are muddled –
their teeth sinking into my neck?...

...my zombie arms fall off.

My zombie head feels foul and rotten –
my dead black heart drops out.

My zombie head, alone.

THE SKELETON IN THE BASEMENT

This poem repeats a little sound phrase "tic tic tac" creating a sense of rhythm and building up the tension in the poem. A sound word is called **onomatopoeia**. Have a go at creating a poem that has an onomatopoeic, repeating sound. It could be something like "Squelch, squelch slurp", or "rustle, rustle". I wonder what poems those sounds will inspire you to write.

There's a skeleton in the basement
rattling its bones:
tic tic tac,
it rattles through my home.

There's a skeleton in the basement
and it's prickling my hairs:
tic tic tac,
it rattles up the stairs.

There's a skeleton in the hallway
its foot-bones tap the floor:
tic tic tac,
it rattles to my door.

There's a skeleton a-knocking
shall I let it in?
Tic tic tac.
It makes a deadly din!
It makes a deadly din!
It makes a deadly din!
Tic tic tac.

Should I let it in?

21

SOW DEEP AND DARK

I like the idea of a plant being scary. Can you write a scary plant poem, does your scary plant eat someone? Does it chase someone, or is it just creepy to look at, like the one in this poem?

The label on the packet of seeds
said, "sow deep and dark".

I took earth from between the roots
of a long dead tree,
I filled up an old stone pot
that I had found in a cemetery.

I pushed my finger into the earth
and gasped when a sharp stone cut.
I placed two seeds in the shadowy hole
and piled the earth right up.

I laid the cracked pot in a cupboard.
I closed the creaking door.
The packet said, "wait for three dark nights
and new shoots will tangle and explore!"

Three sleepless nights passed by
during which the cupboard sang
a melody of haunting sounds
made up of creaks and bangs.

On the third night I noticed
the cupboard door start to creak.
A tendril of greenery
had begun to grow and creep.

I took the stone pot out,
roots had widened its cracks,
and curled within the dark earth:
a bud of red and blue and black.

A bud surrounded by tendrils
that forested all around.
A bud that looked so fleshy
and bulbous and round.

I watered it with tears
and sat it on a moonlit sill.
The bud started to flutter
while it made a terrifying shrill.

The skin started to wrinkle
as two fleshy lids started to part.
The flower revealed beneath
caused a hammering in my heart.

No petals were on show,
no sweet scent wafted by.
Instead, I was met with a bloom
of a monstrous, staring eye.

THE GREY LADY

In this poem there are four stanzas, one about seeing the grey lady, one about hearing her, one about feeling her and the last one returns to seeing her again. Could you copy this structure and write a poem with four stanzas that each talk about seeing, hearing and feeling something scary?

Have you seen her?
Have you seen her?
If you see her,
you will fear her.

Have you heard her?
Have you heard her?
Screaming nightly
about her murder!

Have you felt her?
Have you felt her?
A cold hand
upon your shoulder.

Have you seen her?
Have you seen her?
Run away!
Don't look back.

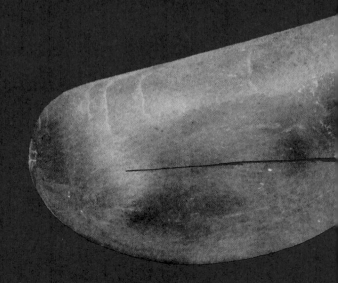

DOWN THE DEEP DARK

This poem takes us on a journey that gets deeper and darker. Write your own creepy
journey poem. You can use repetition as I have done here: repeating certain elements about
how deep and dark each stage of the journey is. You can also use other adjectives.
Maybe each stage of the journey is "cold and foggy" or "misty and wet". Experiment with
some different **adjectives** to get a description that you feel is spooky and unique.

In the old, dark house
there's a deep, dark basement.
Down the deep, dark basement
there are some winding, dark stairs.
Down the winding, dark stairs
there's an old, cavernous pit.
Down the old, cavernous pit
there's a still, dark lake.
In the still, dark lake
there's a wide, dark mouth.
Down the wide, dark mouth
you go tumbling down,
tumbling down,
tumbling down
and you never make a sound.

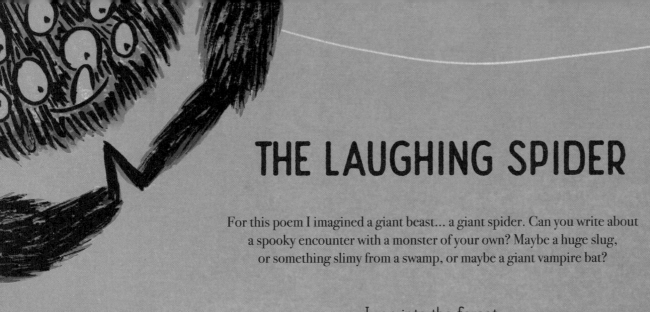

THE LAUGHING SPIDER

For this poem I imagined a giant beast… a giant spider. Can you write about
a spooky encounter with a monster of your own? Maybe a huge slug,
or something slimy from a swamp, or maybe a giant vampire bat?

I ran into the forest,
heard a skittering at my back,
the branches of the trees
all long and thin and black.

The night seemed to stick,
the moonlight seemed to suck,
the skittering got louder
I tripped, face down in muck.

I gathered all the things
fallen from my backpack,
strapped them up tight
like a bulging white egg sack.

My nerves were all abuzz
as the skittering scuttled near,
a clicking of mandibles
wrapped my body in fear.

The thing was ahead of me,
above me and either side.
It swung from the canopy
spun from the corners of my eyes.

It landed ahead of me,
eight legs and eight eyes.
Bigger than a car –
a giant spidery surprise!

I had run out of options,
I had no means to attack.
So, I ran for the beast
and leapt up, upon its back!

Then I tickled it all over,
tickled the fur along its back.
The thing was shocked
and then had a laughing attack.

It giggled and it chortled!
Its legs wobbled and splayed out wide.
The thing laughed so much
"Please stop!" it chuckled and cried.

But I just kept on tickling
until its legs started tickling me too.
We rolled about on the floor
an unlikely tickling crew.

We lay exhausted upon the forest floor:
smiling boy and grinning beast.
And then with one quick sling of silk
he gobbled me up – his laughing feast.

THE THING IN THE SWAMP

What do you imagine might be living is a deep dark swamp?
A giant frog? A foulsome toad? A monstrous leech? Or a thing
composed of slime! Write your very own swamp poem.

At the bottom of the quarry
where the old swamp lies
all bubbling and squelching
like a monster's evil eye.

One child is playing
throwing sticks and stones
the swamp swallows each one
goodbye stick, goodbye stone!

The child keeps on larking
getting closer as he plays.
The swamp seems to sense him
in a dark mysterious way.

The child's foot slips
at the edge of the gurgling pool.
His trainer comes away sticky
covered in monstrous drool.

Thick and black like tar
the trainer is ruined.
The child weeps on the ground
unaware of what the swamp is doing.

Its centre starts to bulge
a bubble of liquorice-ink.
The bubble gets taller,
the bubble starts to think.

It glides across the swamp
becoming more like a man.
A body of darkness –
no features, or fingers or hands.

Just a rough man-like sludge
that slithers ever near.
The child is sad about his trainer
the child doesn't hear...

...the swamp's gentle sludging
as it oozes behind his back.
The child doesn't see
the swamp crouch for the attack.

But no attack comes
it just raises a drooping arm.
The sludge upon the trainer
sloughs off like it's been charmed.

It rejoins the goo
now looming behind the boy.
It leaves his trainer spotless,
replacing his tears with joy.

Bleary-eyed the boy turns
having heard a squelching pop.
But there is nothing to be seen
except the dark, silent slop.

The boy gets up to leave,
stagers quietly to his home.
His trainers newly cleaned,
the swamp left sad and alone.

THE PRANKING GHOST

If you were a ghost what pranks would you pull? Could you write a poem
about all the funny things you would get up to as a pranking ghost?

I make your doors creak
with a ghostly moan.
I make your phone ring –
leave you with the dialling tone.

I open all the cupboards
and run up and down the stairs.
I make the cat hiss –
make your dog bark and stare.

I'm the pranking ghost
and this is what I do.
I rearrange your furniture –
cover your walls in greenish goo.

I make every shadow scary
from the corner of your eye.
Fill your loo with ghastly smells
and fill your socks with buzzing flies.

I'm a gagging ghoulie,
I'm a jackanaping vision,
I'm a wicked wraith,
I'm an aping apparition.

DOG IN THE MOONLIGHT

This type of poem is called a **renga**. Each verse of a renga is made up of a **tanka** poem. A tanka has 5 syllables in the first line, 7 syllables in the second line, 5 syllables in the third line and the two last lines have 7 syllables each.

A nice way of writing a renga is to take it in turns with a friend to write a tanka for each verse. The more tankas you add, the longer your renga will become.

Dog in the moonlight,
staring across my estate,
howling a sad song
reminding me of something –
bites into my memory.

Dog in the moonlight,
his baying getting louder.
I close my curtains
dig down into my duvet
and dream of sharp gnashing teeth.

Dog in the moonlight
scratching hard at my window.
His howl is now words
growling a dagger-tooth threat
from an all too human face.

CLOMP!

Many creepy tales involve disembodied body parts such as the hand, Thing, in *The Addams Family*. Could you write a poem about a disembodied body part? Maybe an ear, or a nose, or a foot or maybe even an eye.

It was the clomping of footsteps...
Clomp!
Clomp!
Clomp!
...from the cellar below,
that woke me.
As the storm jolted and jumped.

The power was out
all was dark.
The running stairs lolled out ahead of me,
as the wind kicked at the windows.

First step,
creak!
Second step,
creak!
Third step,
CLOMP – from above!

The carpet was so cold
it felt wet,
as I climbed the jagged tread of the stairs,
as the rain nailed the house's bones.

The attic door swung on its joints
as the storm heel-toed
around the roof's tapping tiles.

In the lightning-lit flashes
of the attic's window
I saw it...
a single withered leg
skin dried and tight,
nails long and black.
Hopping towards me...
Clomp!
Clomp!
CLOMP!

A LOT LIKE ME

This creepy, cellar poem is a **pantoum**. Pantoums have two rhymes throughout. The second and fourth lines of each verse are repeated as the third and first lines respectively in the following verse. In the fourth verse we also get a repeat of lines one and three from verse one as they become lines two and four. Could you copy this structure and make your own cellar based pantoum?

"Stay out of the cellar", say Mum and Dad
as they bolt the door with a rusty padlock.
"There is something down there – horrid and bad".
Their warning chills, I am silent with shock.

Their warning chills, I am silent with shock.
I press my ear to the cellar and carefully listen
as they bolt the door with another padlock.
I hear a noise, my eyes start to glisten.

I hear a noise, my eyes start to glisten.
The thing's wailing cry sounds a lot like me!
I press my ear to the cellar and carefully listen
I hear myself snarling, I beg to be free!

I hear myself snarling, I beg to be free!
"Stay out of the cellar", say Mum and Dad.
The thing's wailing cry sounds a lot like me!
"There is something down there – horrid and bad".

THE SMELLERS

This poem is a **villanelle**. Like the pantoum it has two rhymes throughout and each verse ends with a repetition of either the first or third line from verse one. Those two repeated lines then come together to end the final four-line verse. The repetition creates a nice sense of tension when used for a creepy poem like this. Write your own villanelle about hearing something getting closer.

Snuffling around the back of your head
a steady, rhythmic, creeping inhalation.
A whispering of snivelling dread.

They smell the living, they do, the dead!
You smell so different from their stagnation.
Snuffling around the back of your head.

You hear them as you lie awake in bed.
A sucking of air of too long a duration.
A whispering of snivelling dread.

You try to make out what the whisperer said,
but there are no known words in this iteration –
snuffling around the back of your head.

"Deter with foul smells", is what you have read
in an ancient tome of crumbling pagination.
A whispering of snivelling dread.

You choose to not wash, to stink like a deathbed
until you reek with an eye-watering emanation.
But still... snuffling around the back of your head:
a whispering of snivelling dread.

PENNY BRIDGE

Trolls have long been associated with bridges. Write a poem that describes a troll living under a bridge near to where you live. Is it a nice troll or a bad troll, does it have a name? What does it eat? What does it like to do on the weekends?

Throw a penny
over Penny Bridge.
Pay the troll
his penny toll.

Throw a penny
over Penny Bridge
for the troll
to stay below.

Throw a penny
over Penny Bridge.
Stop the troll
from eating you whole!

Stop the troll
from eating you whole.

Stop the troll
from eating you
whole.

If you forget
to pay the toll.

The troll will rise up
from below.

A WITCHY NIGHT

Can you draw this witch-tastic ball?

Witchy fingers.
Witchy toes.
Witchy wart.
Witchy nose.
Witchy hat
upon your head.
Witchy dreams
in a witchy bed!

Witchy wakes
on a witchy night.
Witchy cat on a broom.
Witchy cauldron.
Witchy spoon.
Witchy shoes
on your feet.
Witchy spells.
Wow!
Witchy treats.

Witchy laugh
all cackle cackle.
Witchy mog –
raised hackles.
Witchy dance
on a witchy night.
Witchy party.
Witchy fright.

Witches here and witches there
witches soaring through the air.
Witches conjuring all sorts of riches,
collecting frogs from muddy ditches.

Witches together on All Hallows' Eve –
a ball like you would not believe.

For all you little poets out there
who like a little poetic scare. – J.C.

For Illi and Poe, my terrifying hounds of love. – D.G-B.

Spooky Poems Aloud © 2024 Quarto Publishing plc.
Text © 2024 Joseph Coelho.
Illustrations © 2024 Daniel Gray-Barnett

First published in 2024 by Wide Eyed Editions, an imprint of The Quarto Group.
One Triptych Place, London, SE1 9SH, United Kingdom.
T (0)20 7700 6700 F (0)20 7700 8066 **www.Quarto.com**

The right of Daniel Gray-Barnett to be identified as the illustrator and Joseph Coelho to be identified
as the author of this work has been asserted by them in accordance with the Copyright, Designs and
Patents Act, 1988 (United Kingdom).

A catalogue record for this book is available from the British Library.

ISBN 978-0-7112-8739-6
eISBN 978-0-7112-8742-6

The illustrations were created with traditional and digital media
Set in Nature Spirit, Bodoni and Print Clearly

Published by Debbie Foy and Georgia Buckthorn
Designed by Myrto Dimitrakoulia
Commissioned and edited by Lucy Brownridge
Production by Dawn Cameron

Manufactured in Guangdong, China TT052024
9 8 7 6 5 4 3 2 1